Flour...sugar...
Margarine!
Everybody,
Let's begin!

Measure the dry.
Pile it high.

Stir the batter.
No time for chatter.

CINNAMON

Go...go...go!
Roll the dough.

A gingerbread house
Is work for a mouse.

Wait 'til it's cool.
That's the rule.

Carry a wall.
Don't let it fall.

Let's spread it thick
And make it stick.

Decorate the door.
No icing on the floor!

Smell the breeze—
Spearmint trees!

Peppermint candy,
Cinnamon!